The Adventures of
Daisy & Yogi

Written by Daisy, Illustrated by Yogi, and translated by Linn Caroleo

ALWAYS ENJOY THE JOURNEY.

Daisy

+ Yogi

XXOO
WAG MORE,
BARK LESS

In the Forest

My name is Daisy.

I am Daisy the Dog.

My fur is dark colored.

I have a big nose.

I use my nose to smell everything.

I have a little brother named Yogi. His fur is lighter in color than mine. I like the way he smells, kind of like nuts. But he drools a lot. He makes big puddles of drool. Sometimes I think his drool smells like fish. If you accidentally step in his drool you will slip.
I like Yogi.

We live in a house in the woods. There are lots of animals outside, and we watch through the window. If we are let out, Yogi likes to chase squirrels, birds or rabbits, but he never catches any. I can smell when a fox has visited and sometimes we find fox poop. We like our house. We live with two people.

Yogi and I like to play fight. I always win, because I am quicker even though he is stronger. Mostly we play fight inside, but that can upset the humans. So when we are play fighting one of the humans usually lets us go outside.

When we are outside we go on adventures together. Today we go into the forest where it smells like dirt, fir trees and grass. And today, there is a faint odor of deer.

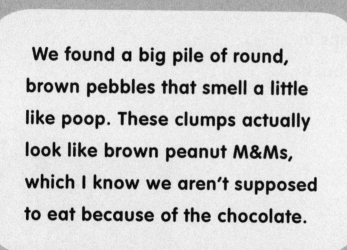

We found a big pile of round, brown pebbles that smell a little like poop. These clumps actually look like brown peanut M&Ms, which I know we aren't supposed to eat because of the chocolate.

But Yogi ate a bunch of those clumps anyway. He said they tasted yummy to him. I smelled his breath and it's stinky. I don't think our owners will like that Yogi ate those round lumps in the forest. We better go back home now.

When we got back home Yogi said his tummy hurt. Then he suddenly threw up on the rug. His barf smelled like deer poop, dirt and of course the sour smell of throw up. He looked very sick. I felt bad for him. And he felt bad for making a mess on the rug. Our human thought we had been eating kidney beans. But we can't talk, so we couldn't tell her it was deer poop that we found in the forest. She cleaned it up and said that we needed to take a time out.

After the rug was cleaned it smelled strongly of soap. That is not my favorite smell. But we sat on the rug anyway and calmed down. Yogi felt better and his tummy was ready for our next meal. He loves to eat. When Yogi is happy he wags his tail a lot. I like it when he wags.

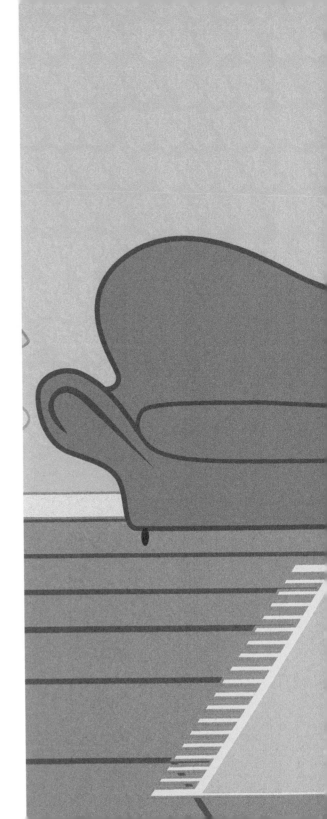

In the Woods

After a while we looked out the window again and we saw a rabbit in front of the house. Yogi got all excited, because he likes to try and chase rabbits. But once we got outside the rabbit was gone, so we went on another adventure into the deep woods.

It is very nice to have a little brother,
who is also my friend and playmate.
He is never scared when we go into
the woods alone. Suddenly there is
an incredible odor in the air. We both
raise our noses and sniff. It's a very,
very strong scent. It's sharp, smelly,
stinky and musty all at the same time.
We have not smelled this smell before,
so we need to investigate it.

Out of the blue, we see a black and white animal that sort of looks like a kitty-cat. This animal is walking through the trees, so we decide to chase it. We run after the black and white animal. Without warning, from the back of the animal, comes a spray that hits Yogi in the face. The smell is horrible. He whines and his eyes water from the terrible stench.

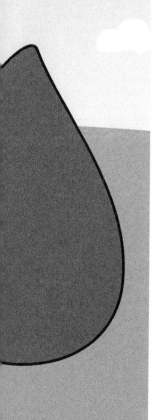

We run back home to our humans, not knowing what the smell is. They immediately put us in the tub and start talking about something called 'skunk'. I guess the animal we chased was a skunk. They sure do smell awful. Yogi has soapsuds on his nose. After the skunk adventure we need a nap, so we go inside.

Adventure Three:

By the Pond

When we wake up from our nap, we look outside and see a fox and a squirrel. And a bird flying overhead. Since we are rested we are ready for another adventure, but this time we'll go through the forest and over to the pond.

As we go through the forest I can smell
pine needles, dirt, moss and daisies.
It is cooler in here among the trees,
because it is shady.

The pond is so pretty. It smells like water and mud.
Around the edge of the pond there are big rocks.
Yogi loves to swim, but today he says he wants to
explore the rocks near the pond. There is a slightly
sour smell in the air, I wonder what that is from.

All of a sudden one of the rocks near the shore starts moving and the sour smell becomes stronger. Yogi immediately chases the moving thing. Watch out! There are long pointy things sticking out of its back. Oh no! Yogi howls in pain and he has some of those sharp things sticking out of his nose.

We run back home with our tails between our legs. We are off to our veterinarian. We are both scared to go to the doctor, but our owner can't take out the pointy things in Yogi's nose. Those things are called quills. Yogi shakes as he sits on the table in the examination room. He is scared and asks me if I think it's going to hurt. But I don't know, because this has never happened to me. The animal we chased is called a porcupine.

After the veterinarian takes the quills out of Yogi's nose, he gets a band-aid on it. I'm glad Yogi is ok, because I love my little brother. Yogi and I go on adventures together and we chase things. When we are together we both wag our tails.

The End
(for now)

Daisy

Yogi

CPSIA information can be obtained
at www.ICGtesting.com
Printed in the USA
LVOW02s2232200116

471416LV00001B/1/P